LADYBIRD BOOKS

UK | USA | Canada | Ireland | Australia | India | New Zealand | South Africa

Ladybird Books is part of the Penguin Random House group of companies
whose addresses can be found at global.penguinrandomhouse.com.
Published by Penguin Random House Children's: 80 Strand, London WC2R ORL, UK
Penguin Random House Australia Pty Ltd: 707 Collins Street, Melbourne, VIC 3008
Penguin Random House New Zealand: 67 Apollo Drive, Rosedale, Auckland 0632

www.penguin.co.uk   www.puffin.co.uk   www.ladybird.co.uk

First published 2017
002

This book copyright © Astley Baker Davies Ltd/Entertainment One UK Ltd 2017
Adapted by Lauren Holowaty

This book is based on the TV series *Peppa Pig*.
Peppa Pig is created by Neville Astley and Mark Baker.
Peppa Pig © Astley Baker Davies Ltd/Entertainment One UK Ltd 2003.
www.peppapig.com

Printed in China
A CIP catalogue record for this book is available from the British Library
ISBN: 978-0-241-29461-1

All correspondence to:
Ladybird Books
Penguin Random House Children's
80 Strand, London WC2R ORL

Peppa's Holiday Post

Granny and Grandpa Pig are getting ready to go on holiday.
"Where are you going?" asks Peppa.
"It's a mystery," replies Grandpa Pig. "We'll send you clues
and you can guess where we are!"
"Ooooh!" gasps Peppa excitedly. "I love mysteries."

"It's time for us to go to the airport,"
says Grandpa, getting into the car.

"See you soon, little ones!"
says Granny Pig, winking.
"Look out for the clues."
"We will!" replies Peppa.

A few days later, a letter arrives at Peppa and George's house.
"It has our names on it, George!" says Peppa, delighted.
"It must be from Granny and Grandpa on their mystery holiday.
Let's open it now!"

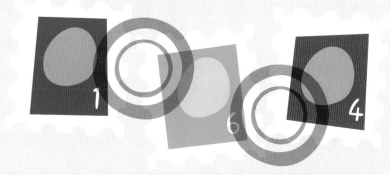

To Peppa and George Pig
The Little House
Top of the Hill

Open me to find clue number one!

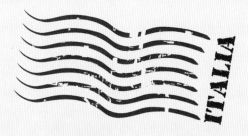

Peppa and George open the envelope with Mummy and Daddy Pig.
"There's a menu inside," says Peppa. "But where is it from?"
"Let me take a look," says Daddy Pig.
Daddy Pig starts to read out the menu. "Pizza, spaghetti . . . hmm . . ."

"Where do you think it's from, Daddy?" asks Peppa.
"I don't know," replies Daddy Pig, pointing at the menu.
"But this is what I would like for dinner!"
"Hee! Hee!" giggle Peppa and George.

The next day, another letter arrives for Peppa and George . . .

AIRMAIL

To Peppa and George Pig
The Little House
Top of the Hill

Wear me – I'm clue number two!

ITALIA

PLEASE DO NOT BEND

PLEASE DO NOT BEND

"Oooh, what lovely sunglasses," says Mummy Pig, smiling.
"Granny and Grandpa sent them to us," explains Peppa.
"I see," says Mummy Pig. "I like the flags. I wonder if that's
a clue about where Granny and Grandpa Pig are."

Peppa and George race off to look
at their sunglasses in the mirror.
"A green, white and red flag,"
says Peppa. "Which country
is it from, George?"
George doesn't know.
He just laughs at
the silly glasses.

Just then, Mr Zebra, the postman,
arrives with yet another letter . . .

To Peppa and George Pig
The Little House
Top of the Hill

Open me to find clue number three!

Inside the third envelope is a phrase book.
"The words are in another language," says Daddy Pig.
"George, can you say *chau*?"
"Meoww?" says George.
"What about *spa – ghe – tti*?" asks Daddy Pig.

ciao

spaghetti

pizza

"Pee-getty!" says George proudly. "Hee, hee!"

The next morning, Peppa and George still haven't guessed where Granny and Grandpa Pig are. When they hear the post coming, they race to the door.

"I wonder what's inside this one?" asks Peppa, picking up the envelope and shaking it.

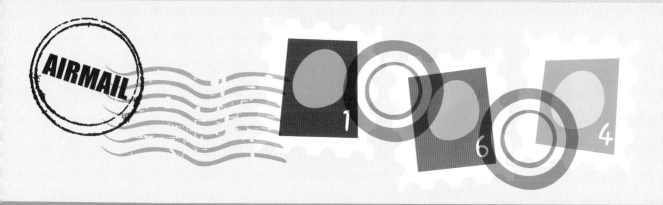

To Peppa and George Pig
The Little House
Top of the Hill

Look at me VERY closely!

"Wow!" cries Peppa, peering inside the envelope. "Postcards!"
"It looks like Granny and Grandpa Pig are somewhere with big, old buildings," says Mummy Pig. "Can you guess where that might be?"

"I know!" shouts Peppa. "Are they at the Eiffel Tower in France?"

"That's a great guess, Peppa. But France's flag is blue, white and red, not like the one on George's glasses." "We need more clues," says Peppa.

Just then, there's a *PLOP* as another letter lands on the mat. "I think that's one now, Peppa," says Mummy Pig. "Let's go and see!"

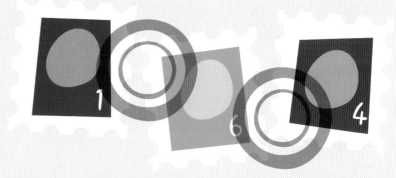

To Peppa and George Pig
The Little House
Top of the Hill

Draw me – I'm clue number five!

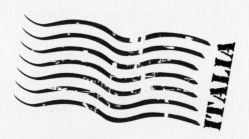

"It's a map!" cries Peppa, pulling clue
number five out of its envelope.
"But it's not finished."
"Maybe *you* can finish it, Peppa," says
Mummy Pig. "Try joining the dots."

"This map looks like one of my boots!"
says Peppa, when she finishes.
"Hee! Hee!" says George.

"What can you see on the map?" Mummy Pig asks Peppa. "There's an **X**," Peppa replies. "Aaaargh! Maybe we can find some treasure there," she adds in her best Pirate Peppa voice.

ROMA
X

"Or maybe that's where Granny and Grandpa Pig are?" suggests Mummy Pig.

"Yes!" replies Peppa. "I think we need our detective hats and magnifying glasses to look closely at the map."
"Yippee!" cheers George, running off to the dressing-up box.
George loves dressing up as a detective.

Peppa and George are ready to be detectives, and to solve Granny and Grandpa Pig's holiday mystery.

"This is where Granny and Grandpa Pig are," says Peppa, pointing to the map on the fridge. "We just need to find out where that is!"

"Well, it's somewhere where they have pizza,"
begins Daddy Pig. "And . . ."
"Pee-getty!" adds George, holding the phrase bool

"And where they have big, old buildings,"
says Mummy Pig, looking at the postcards.
"With a green, white and red flag."
"And the country looks like my boot,"
says Peppa. "So . . ."

But, just as Peppa is about to guess,
another letter arrives . . .

To Peppa and George Pig
The Little House
Top of the Hill

I'm the final clue — use me!

Peppa opens the envelope. She pulls out a passport and a ticket to . . .
"Italy!" she cheers. "Granny and Grandpa are in Italy."
"And now *we* are going there, too," says Mummy Pig, opening
another envelope with tickets inside.
"Yippee!" cheers Peppa.
"Yummy!" cheers Daddy Pig, still looking at the menu.

Peppa, George, Mummy, Daddy,
Granny and Grandpa Pig are all
on holiday in Italy.
"I love holidays!" says Peppa.
"Especially mystery ones."

"Miss-tree pee-getty!" says George, holding up a forkful of spaghetti and hiding behind it! "Ha! Ha! George!" says Peppa. Everyone loves holidays!

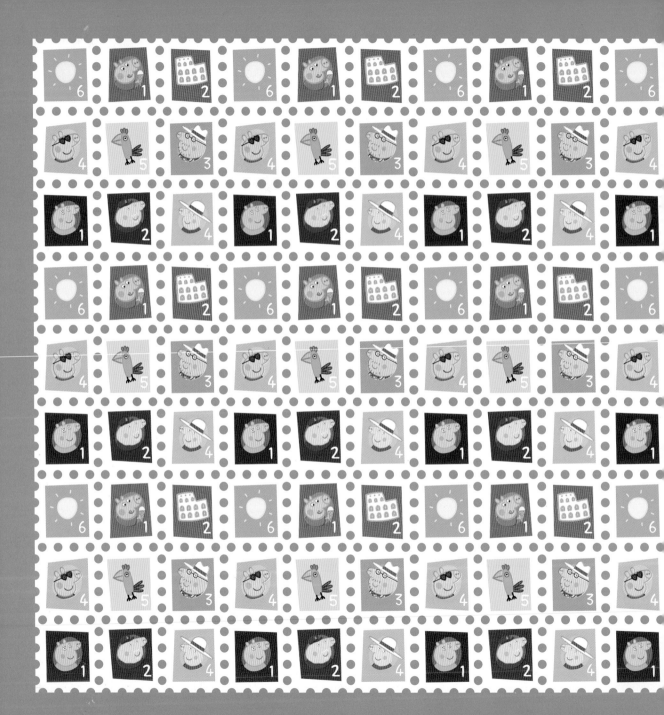